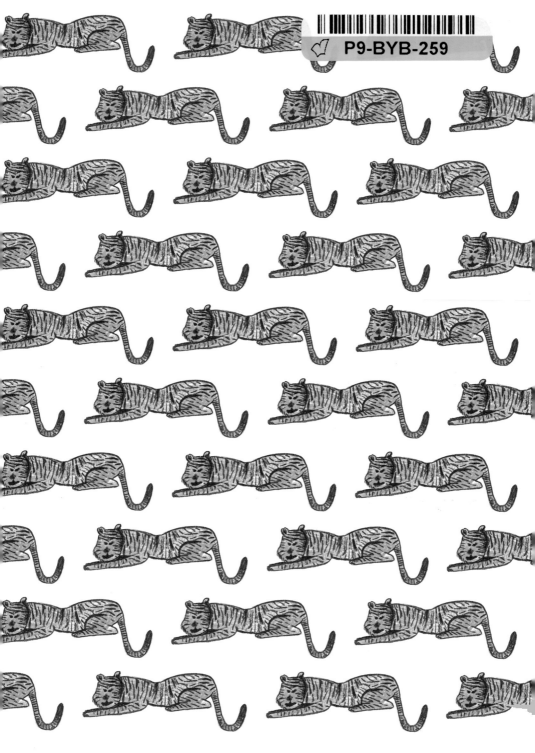

Soda Pop

Soda Pop

Barbro Lindgren

Illustrated by Lisen Adbåge

Translated by Sarah Death

GECKO PRESS

This edition first published in 2017 by Gecko Press
PO Box 9335, Wellington 6141, New Zealand
info@geckopress.com

English language edition © Gecko Press Ltd 2017
Translation © Sarah Death 2017
Illustrations © Lisen Adbåge 2017

Original title: *Loranga* Text © Barbro Lindgren, first published by Rabén & Sjögren,
Sweden, in 1970. Published by agreement with Rabén & Sjögren Agency.

Distributed in the United States and Canada by Lerner Publishing Group,
www.lernerbooks.com
Distributed in the United Kingdom by Bounce Sales and Marketing,
www.bouncemarketing.co.uk
Distributed in Australia by Scholastic Australia, www.scholastic.com.au
Distributed in New Zealand by Upstart Distribution, www.upstartpress.co.nz

The cost of this translation was defrayed by a subsidy
from the Swedish Arts Council, gratefully acknowledged.

Edited by Penelope Todd
Design and typesetting by Katrina Duncan
Printed in China by Everbest Printing Co Ltd,
an accredited ISO 14001 & FSC certified printer

ISBN hardback: 978-1-776570-10-2 (USA)
ISBN paperback: 978-1-776570-11-9

For more curiously good books, visit www.geckopress.com

Contents

Soda Pop, Mazarin and Dartanyong   1

Tigers on the Way   6

Hotdogs and Bed Munching   14

Soda Pop Looks for a Job   24

The Championship   33

The Cushiest Jail in the World   40

Mister Dartanyong, Famous Flying Trapeze Artist   50

Gustav the Robber Drops By   59

A Gold Toilet for Soda Pop   68

Distemper with Scarlet Fever   76

Shocky Poodling and Cripped Weem   84

Scorpion Barrels and Lingonberry Cases   93

Soda Pop, Mazarin and Dartanyong

At first, all you see is trees. Lots of pines and firs, a few rocks and anthills, and last year's needles and pine cones.

Then you spot a few buildings. One, two, three, eleven, twenty of them. Well, only seven, really, if you count the garage and the woodshed, which of course you do.

If you open the door to the biggest, reddest building, you enter a glassed-in porch. It can take a while, by the way, because the door's always getting stuck. You have to yank the handle three times up and down and side to side, while kicking as hard as you can, then maybe it will open.

The next door will certainly open, because it never shuts properly. Through that, you find yourself in a bilious green hall and wonder where to go next. The best idea is straight ahead.

You'll come to a blue room, with blue walls, blue chairs, and blue curtains fluttering at the windows. But under the sofa, there's a small chubby red boy. He has tiny little kind eyes, big red ears, and droopy cheeks.

His name is Mazarin and he's pretty strong, about as strong as you generally are at that age. Other than that, there's nothing out of the ordinary about him. He eats buns, reads comics, and wanders about in the usual way.

If you turn right you come to the kitchen. In there, everything's red. The cupboards and the stove, the curtains, plates, and dishes. The table is round and red, and on the floor underneath is a rather fat and lazy dad. He might be the only thing in the kitchen that isn't red—he's more orange, like orange fizz. And what's more, his name is Soda Pop. Oh, and Soda Pop is a really great dad—he couldn't care less about anything.

If there's a sudden boom that shakes the whole house like a cannon firing, that'll be Soda Pop switching on the radio. He has to have it turned up as loud as it will go, or it hurts his ears. And it has to be pop music, or it makes his tummy ache.

There are a few other rooms in the house. A fiery red one, a green, a mauve, and a black one. Soda Pop's always fancied a gold room, too, but as long as gold is so expensive, that'll have to wait.

So let's leave Mazarin under the sofa munching buns and Soda Pop under the kitchen table crooning pop songs, and sneak back out through the glassed-in porch to look at the other buildings.

No one lives in the dilapidated old shed to the right. Just a few earwigs and dead bumblebees. But then there's the woodshed, where Soda Pop's dad lives. He's pretty old and dilapidated too. He lives alone in the woodshed so other people's germs can't jump out and grab him. Not that it seems to help because he's always getting sick, all the same. They call him Dartanyong, which someone said is Spanish for feeble. When he isn't too unwell, he compiles charts to help him remember everything.

Behind the woodshed there's a fancy rubbish heap, where most of the time you'll find a giraffe, snoring with his head in an old tin can. The giraffe came gangling along years ago, plonked itself down on Soda Pop's rubbish heap, and has been there ever since.

But it wanders off from time to time and eats whatever it can find, scares away the cows, and careens around the fields, bellowing. One thing it gobbled up was the garage roof. The whole caboodle, every single roof tile, and a jolly good thing too because there's been so much rain the garage has turned into a swimming pool. Now Mazarin and Soda Pop swim there every day!

Then there's a cowshed and a stable and the remaining cows. Also a barn and a henhouse where a few red and yellow owls live.

That's all the buildings, except of course there's a police station and a very nice jail a few miles away. And there's a hot-doggery selling hotdogs if you have the money for them or something to swap.

And up in the top of a fir tree in the forest lives Dartanyong's grandpa. He's so old he can only make cuckoo noises. At Christmas and on special Sundays, Dartanyong takes him seeds and a few other little treats. And that's really all there is. An old pigsty maybe. A washhouse or two.

Tigers on the Way

There was a bang—boom!—like a cannon. It was Soda Pop cracking a really hard nut left over from last Christmas. The giraffe started up from the rubbish heap and lolloped out into the field of oats, which was flowering like mad. Mazarin crammed the last crumbs of bun into his mouth, blinked his ginormously kind eyes, hauled himself up off the floor, and went outside.

He went to the garage, clambered up the ladder, and sat on the edge of the roof, absentmindedly kicking his feet in the water. Way down at the bottom he could see the glint of Soda Pop's car, with little schools of herring swimming right through it because the windows were open. It was so quiet and peaceful. The only sounds were the pike squeaking in the water and the occasional loud crunch as Soda Pop cracked a nut in the kitchen.

Mazarin felt sort of happy sitting there. The sun was rising and it warmed his ears so gloriously.

But somewhere beyond the pikey squeaks and the nutty cracks was a faint hum. It didn't sound quite like the wind or quite like a plane: not quite like anything in particular.

The hum came closer and closer, with lots of whining, howling, and growling. Mazarin stood up and stared across the fields. On the horizon, what looked like a cloud of smoke was slowly advancing.

"Must be tigers," Mazarin said to himself. "A whole swarm of them." So he shouted to Soda Pop that tigers were on the way and Soda Pop came out like a shot because he was crazy about tigers, or so he thought.

The black cloud was fast closing in on them. Soon the growls were loud and clear, the humming and buzzing too.

And then the huge swarm of tigers was arriving, by leaps and bounds—there must have been a thousand of them. The whole garden was brimming with tigers! Twenty or thirty threw themselves into the swimming pool and at least seven hundred poured into the barn, where the doors had been left wide open.

Mazarin ran inside as fast as he could and hid in the kitchen until the worst of the growling was over.

"Scaredy cat," shouted Soda Pop.

Then the tigers leapt on him and all you could see was a tangle of limbs and teeth.

Mazarin found his army knife and crept back outside to rescue poor Soda Pop.

But there was no need, because he found Soda Pop sitting on the side of the swimming pool, whistling and kicking his legs in the water. There was no sign of tigers.

"What a scaredy cat, whipping off for an army knife just because a few tigers happen to show up," said Soda Pop.

"I thought that if they were gobbling you up I could stab them and make them let go."

"Ah, but that would have hurt them," said Soda Pop. "Anyway, these aren't as dangerous as most tigers. This lot have a softer bite."

"So where have they all gone?" asked Mazarin.

"They whooshed into the barn so I closed the door, quick as a flash—and bam, they were mine," said Soda Pop.

"And mine," said Mazarin.

"But mostly mine," said Soda Pop with a cross-eyed stare. "So that's that, but I need to cool off a bit now. Good job I've got my bathrobe on, the water feels a bit chilly." Soda Pop dived ears first into the pool with his bathrobe flying behind him like a giant scarf.

He swam four laps for practice, because he couldn't really swim at all, but then he collided with a pike, which put him off his stroke. He struggled out onto the side and sat beside Mazarin.

"Those wretched pike," he said. "That's my fourth collision in two days."

As they sat listening to the tiger growls from the barn, big bubbles began to rise in the swimming pool.

"Whatever kind of bubbles those are, they're not pikey ones," said Soda Pop. "Let's dive down and investigate."

Down they went, as straight as two arrows, to the car glinting at the bottom. There were tigers in it! There must have been thirty, squeezed in any old how and eating salami sandwiches that had been left there after a picnic.

Quite a few of the tigers had faded in the water. Some had lost their ears, and their tails were all limp and bent.

Then Soda Pop and Mazarin had to hurry back up to breathe, or they would have drowned.

"We'll dive back down and poke them in the tummy to make them come up," said Soda Pop.

So down they went again like a couple of arrows and poked the tigers in the tummy.

It worked a treat. The tigers swam straight up to the surface and jumped splashily down onto the lawn.

"Hmph, back to the forest, you lot! You look plain daft with those loose ears and everything," said Soda Pop.

"Too right. Decrepitigers aren't worth having," said Mazarin, putting down his army knife. "They look like old telliphones!"

"Ergh, yes, go in and get our sticks and we'll shoot them," said Soda Pop.

Mazarin dashed in for the sticks and they fired away as if they were machine guns until all the tigers had vanished back into the forest.

Then, with a faint creak, the door of the woodshed slowly opened and there stood Dartanyong, blinking in the sun.

"Please stop all that dreadful shooting," he squeaked, "it makes my knees swell up something chronic."

"You look pretty well apart from that," shouted Soda Pop, aiming his stick at him.

"No, today it's really bad and, what's more, my little toe's jammed up so I can't even wiggle it."

But as usual, Soda Pop wasn't listening.

"Glad to hear you're feeling so well. Do you know what I think you should do? Go over to the barn, open the door and shut your eyes, and we'll all have a lot of fun!"

Dartanyong gave him a suspicious look.

"As long as no germs jump out at me," he said.

"No, there won't be any of that, I guarantee it." Soda Pop tittered.

Being almost as nosy as he was poorly, Dartanyong started for the barn with shuffling steps.

Soda Pop burst into such guffaws that he kept falling over, but Mazarin rushed back inside for his army knife.

"Phooey, if they're dangerous we'll throw old letters at them and knock their teeth out," chirped Soda Pop.

Dartanyong had a buzzing in his head most of the time, so he couldn't hear the tiger growls as well as the others did. But from outside the barn door he realized there was some sort of noise inside.

"Are the owls choking on something?" he asked, turning the door handle.

The army knife quivered in Mazarin's hand. Waiting out on the grass, Soda Pop squirmed and scrabbled and screeched with laughter.

Then the door creaked open and eight terrified cows came tearing out with their tails in the air.

They'd forgotten they even had cows.

Dartanyong was so scared that he slammed the door shut and slumped to the ground with a thud.

"I almost got trampled," he puffed. "It was a jolly close thing. My little toe was almost trampled!"

And he lay down and shut his eyes so he wouldn't get a temperature.

"Open the door again, man, so we can have some real fun," said Soda Pop.

But Dartanyong said no: that cow stampede had scared him stiff. His head buzz was much worse than before.

"Oh boy, oh boy, if he knew what we've got in there, his whole head would explode!" hooted Soda Pop.

Dartanyong didn't hear a word because the tigers had started to roar.

Soda Pop found an old newspaper, rolled it into a trumpet, and yelled through it, right into Dartanyong's ear.

"How about going into the barn tomorrow then? Let's say nine o'clock, Dartanyong. See you then. Good night, good night, sleep well!"

He gave Dartanyong a jokey bash over the head with the newspaper. Dartanyong saw stars as he limped lopsidedly back into his woodshed.

"Don't you think you're a bit hard on Dartanyong, Soda Pop?" Mazarin asked.

"Phooey, he likes being bashed over the head with papers, he's told me that," said Soda Pop.

"Are you going in to see the tigers now?" Mazarin asked.

"No, are you crazy—they're lethal. Let's go and have something to eat," said Soda Pop.

Hotdogs and
Bed Munching

"Let's have something really quick," said Soda Pop. "No boiling or frying or messing about."

"S'pose we could have ice cream, as usual," said Mazarin.

"Well said." Soda Pop clapped his hands.

"And a slice of bread each with a squirt of fish paste."

"Perfect!" Soda Pop exclaimed. "How come I have such a genius for a son?" He turned on the pop music as loud as it would go without shaking the house to pieces. "A bit of pop music never spoilt any food that I know of." He sat contentedly at the kitchen table and spread out his biggest newspaper.

"Where shall I put the ice cream, then?" asked Mazarin.

"Anywhere you like except on the comic strips," said Soda Pop. Mazarin looked out of the window. "So the cows ran away."

"Doesn't matter," said Soda Pop. "Tigers are much more fun."

"As long they don't eat us up," said Mazarin.

Just then they noticed a little old man standing outside.

A minute or two later, the man came into the kitchen.

"I have a question," he said. "Do you keep red owls here? If so, they're in the habit of sleeping in my mailbox. And it's got to stop because there's no room for my mail."

"We have two red owls," said Soda Pop, "one big one and one little. And three yellow owls too."

"Well, I couldn't care less about the yellow ones, but I'm going to set the police on the red ones," said the man. A red owl had once bitten his big toe and he'd detested them ever since.

"Can I offer you a bit of ice cream and fish paste?" Soda Pop asked.

The cross old man wasn't eager. "Just a small helping, with a little dollop of fish paste on the very top."

He had a quick read of Soda Pop's comic strips and gave a snort. "Useless, the comic strips these days," he said. "A bit more of that one with the flying trapeze artist wouldn't go amiss."

As he finished his ice cream and slurped down the last of his fish paste he remembered the red owls and got really cross.

"Snoring away in my mailbox," he sputtered. "Prison's the only place for them. If I had a telliphone on me, I'd ring the police right now."

"Go and look in our barn instead," Soda Pop suggested, "and you'll find something fantastic."

The cross old man wasted no time heading to the barn. But

15

when he heard all the savage growling, he didn't feel like it any more and dashed back into the kitchen.

"It must be full of tigers," he panted.

Soda Pop told him that was right. Chock-full of tigers. Each one more dangerous than the last. If he liked he could stick his head through the window. They'd charge a gold coin for a look!

The cross old man got so cross that he charged off home in a cloud of dust.

Towards evening, the growling grew even louder. Poor Dartanyong lay quaking in bed with his rubber boots on, thinking it was thunder.

"I suppose they want food," said Soda Pop.

He and Mazarin pressed their ears to the barn door.

"Hotdogs," said Mazarin.

"We'd better get some right away," said Soda Pop. "We'll take the giraffe."

They found the giraffe on the rubbish heap as usual, asleep with his head in the tin can.

"Up you get, giraffe, you old bag of bones, we're going for hotdogs!" yelled Soda Pop.

The giraffe leapt up because he knew what hotdogs were.

They soon reached the shop, which was crammed from floor to ceiling with hotdogs. They bought a thousand but when it was time to pay, Soda Pop had no money on him.

"I expect we can come and pay another day. I have loads of money at home," said Soda Pop.

The hotdog man looked puzzled. "Are you telling me you keep enough money at home to buy a thousand hotdogs?"

"Ye-e-e-s, I'm sure I do," said Soda Pop. "For instance, yesterday I spotted a hundred down the back of the bathroom radiator."

"And there's loads of money under the stove that we lost when we were playing banks," said Mazarin.

"Take the hotdogs then, and I'll give you an invoice," said the hotdog man.

Soda Pop and Mazarin loaded the hotdogs into bags and

heaved them up onto the giraffe's back, and they galloped home again.

Soda Pop opened the barn door just far enough to push the bags inside and locked it again in a flash. Soon afterwards the growling turned to purring. Then the tigers fell asleep, draped over each other in an untidy heap.

Dartanyong could relax at last, so he took off his rubber boots and sat on top of the woodpile outside the woodshed.

"Why don't you go into the barn at long last?" said Soda Pop. "Now the thunder's stopped."

"Suppose I might." Dartanyong limped across to the barn.

While Soda Pop went into his usual fits of laughter, Mazarin dashed indoors for the army knife.

Dartanyong blew on the key for luck before he unlocked the door, pulled it open and went in. For some time there wasn't a sound, only deathly quiet.

After two minutes, Soda Pop's fits of laughter grew strained, and after four minutes, he and Mazarin had faces as white as paper bags and were quivering like aspen leaves.

"We can bury him under the oak tree next to Gramps, where the violets come up in spring," whispered Soda Pop, wiping a tear from his eye.

Just then the door was wrenched open and there stood Dartanyong in the sunshine, hale and hearty and all in one piece. Even his ears were still in place!

"I'm not telling you what was in there," he said mysteriously. "You wouldn't believe me anyway. But they were stripey and they didn't wake up, not even when I poked them with my stick."

"Let me shake your hand. You're the bravest man I know," said Soda Pop.

"Hmph, I was a tiger tamer when I was young," Dartanyong said modestly.

Then he went back to the woodshed, got out his best pencil and drew up a tiger chart with lots of columns and rows.

As the afternoon wore on, Mazarin and Soda Pop shuffled into the house and played ice hockey with a couple of old brooms they'd swiped from Dartanyong. They used a squishy orange, and its juice sprayed the walls whenever Soda Pop gave it a good

wallop. Mazarin was Canada, Soda Pop was Russia, and all the doors were goals. Soda Pop was so shameless that even though he was the dad he kept scoring goals. In the end Mazarin got a bad case of the grumps and went to lie under a sofa. He didn't care about ice hockey any more.

Then it was evening and when they came to say goodnight, they realized the giraffe was missing, because the rubbish heap was empty.

"Well, he's only got himself to blame," said Soda Pop. They closed the door and went up to bed. But when Mazarin looked for his nightshirt under the pillow, he saw that the pillow was gone, and the quilt and mattress too. In fact, the whole bed was gone. There was nothing left but a pile of dust on the floor.

Soda Pop's bed had also vanished without trace. There was nothing but dust there, either. In fact, Mazarin and Soda Pop were both quite relieved because they found lying in bed asleep pretty boring.

"We might as well give up sleeping," said Soda Pop. "Let's go to the garage and take a dip instead."

They put on their bathrobes at once, and their longest scarves too, because it was a chilly evening.

But when they reached the pool, they found the water full of owls splashing and pike messing about at the surface.

"We'd better come back later," said Soda Pop, and they climbed down again.

The light was on in Dartanyong's window so they knocked and went in. Dartanyong sat there drawing lines with a ruler.

On every other line he wrote *Thursday* and on the lines in between he wrote *tiger*, then he wrote down his pulse rate and temperature and when the sun rose and everything else besides.

"You didn't happen to see our beds, Mazarin's and my mine, sauntering past?" asked Soda Pop. "Someone must have stolen them if they didn't run away by themselves."

Dartanyong shut his eyes and thought about it, shaking his head from time to time to reduce the buzz.

After a long pause, he said, "Now you come to mention it, I saw the giraffe running off with a bed or two in his mouth, a good hour ago."

Then he went quiet again, writing figures up and down and across his chart.

"Were there mattresses and things?" asked Soda Pop. "Pillows and quilts and all that?"

Dartanyong was writing *seven seven seven* in three boxes all in a row and didn't answer. His head buzz was going full throttle and he'd already forgotten the giraffe, and the beds and bedcovers.

"Why are you drivelling on about quilts and pillows?" he hissed. "Can't you see I'm making a chart and want to be left in peace? Good afternoon."

And with that, Dartanyong slammed his door, and Soda Pop and Mazarin headed off to the forest to look for the giraffe. It was completely dark outside. The owls were hooting in the henhouse and the trees were pitch black.

As Soda Pop and Mazarin felt their way between the pine trees they heard a crunching up ahead, the sort of noise a giraffe makes when it's crunching away at a standard sort of bed.

They soon reached the top of a hill, where they found the giraffe munching on Soda Pop's bed. It had already finished Mazarin's, leaving only a few scraps of mattress in the moss.

"Bon appetit," said Soda Pop. "Was my nightshirt tasty? I'd dropped some milk chocolate on it."

And then he whacked the giraffe with a bed leg to make sure it didn't get bumptious and think it had done something clever.

On the way home, Mazarin and Soda Pop took things a bit easier. They were in no hurry since they had no beds to sleep in.

It felt very odd not to go to bed. Mazarin was tired and couldn't stop yawning.

"I know, we'll have a dip in the pool," said Soda Pop. So they climbed the ladder and threw themselves in because the owls had gone and the pike had dived down to the bottom.

They floated on their backs and looked up at the stars, and Soda Pop sang pop songs for an hour or two until the giraffe came thundering past and slumped onto the rubbish heap with his head in the tin can.

Then they sloshed into the house with water streaming from their clothes, and fell asleep in the middle of the kitchen floor, where they both slept like logs.

Soda Pop Looks for a Job

The next morning they slept until noon.

They had just picked themselves up off the floor to have a game of broomstick ice hockey when there was a knock at the door and Dartanyong tumbled in. Quick as a flash they threw the brooms under the stove because they actually belonged to him if you wanted to be picky about it.

"Do have a seat," said Soda Pop. "It's been quite a while since your last visit. Allow me to introduce my son Mazarin!"

Dartanyong gave a sniff and perched on the edge of a chair.

"It's so long since I went to see Grandpa," he said. "I was thinking we could take him a few seeds and whatnot. He might be hungry, poor thing."

"Yes, he's bound to be. We haven't been to see him since

Christmas Eve," said Soda Pop. "So I bet he's hungry, and thirsty too."

"If you happen to have beer and a few sunflower seeds we can go over there straight away," said Dartanyong.

Soda Pop hunted out some seeds and beer and stowed them in an old straw hat that had been Dartanyong's, long ago when his head was bigger.

It was easy to find the pine tree where Dartanyong's grandpa lived because, once upon a time, Soda Pop had painted little markers on the trees along the route. It was like a running track, and they raced along like lunatics. They ran so fast that they clean forgot about Dartanyong's grandpa and arrived back home with the seeds and things!

The next time they remembered to stop at the pine tree because Dartanyong had run out of puff.

Also, he was much taken with Soda Pop's food basket.

"What a magnificent basket," he said, over and over. "Such a lovely little brim and everything."

"Yes, it's a good basket," said Soda Pop. He couldn't be bothered explaining everything just then.

Dartanyong's grandpa was so pleased to see him that he crowed like crazy. He was perched on a branch close to the ground so they found him easily.

"Good day to you, Grandpa, how's things?" said Dartanyong. "Are your guts in good working order?"

"Cuck-oo," said Dartanyong's grandpa, and his wings drooped.

"Are you thirsty, Grandpa?" asked Soda Pop.

"Cuck-oo, cuck-oo, cuck-oo!" And he leaped up and down.

"Well, he's thirsty, at least," said Soda Pop, opening a bottle of beer.

After a while, Dartanyong's grandpa hopped down onto Dartanyong's shoulder and whispered to him.

"Eh, can he talk?" said Soda Pop. "What's he saying?"

"He's saying you ought to get a job," said Dartanyong.

"Hah, stirring up trouble, is he?" shouted Soda Pop. "Get a job and ruin the best years of my life!"

"He says everybody else works," said Dartanyong.

"But I have to stay home to play with Mazarin," said Soda Pop. "And who's going to listen to the pop music if I'm not home to do it, you tell me that."

"Now he's saying you have to earn money, like everyone else," said Dartanyong.

"Phooey, I have money strewn around the house. I keep finding coins," said Soda Pop. "Tell him there'll be no more bags of seeds for him if there's going to be all this nagging. Good day to you."

And Soda Pop went striding off.

Back home, Soda Pop and Mazarin sat on the steps and stared into space. Soda Pop was deflated.

"Why should I start working all of a sudden when I haven't had to before?" he grumbled.

The tigers had set up a terrible growling in the barn. They were hungry again, of course.

"We'd better get more hotdogs," said Mazarin.

So they took off to the hotdoggery with the giraffe in tow.

"A thousand hotdogs, please," said Soda Pop.

"Do you have money with you today?" asked the hotdog man.

No, of course they'd forgotten the money.

"But you haven't paid for the last lot yet!"

No, they'd forgotten that as well.

"You'll have to go home for the money. Bye," said the hotdog man.

"Have you seen any large sums of money notes swilling around at home recently?" asked Soda Pop out on the road.

"No, only a few bits of loose change," said Mazarin, "and that hundred down behind the bathroom radiator."

"Oh, what a bore. I suppose I'll have to get a job after all," sighed Soda Pop.

So they took the giraffe and went on for a while. When they

came to a house, they knocked. A red woman with yellow hair came to the door.

"Good day, do you have any work?" asked Soda Pop.

"What sort of thing can you do?" asked the woman.

"I can do anything, and Mazarin can help me."

"What I mean is, what's your trade?"

"Soda Pop's my name," said Soda Pop with a bow. "I'm also a carpenter and a chimney sweep and a plumber. In fact I do everything. I can crack nuts, too. As big as you like. And I can be a caretaker and a tiger tamer, at a pinch."

"Well then, you can be our resident potato peeler," said the woman. "With a room of your own and a separate front door."

"Oh, no thanks," said Soda Pop. "You can peel your old potatoes yourself, and I have front doors at home. If I can't be a sweep, we'll have to leave it."

So they said goodbye and went on their way, and the woman was left standing there, shaking her head.

Then they knocked at the door of a pot-bellied man.

Soda Pop said he could do almost anything in the world except peel potatoes, and he was looking for a job so he could make money and get rich.

The pot-bellied man was delighted because he needed a housekeeper who was a good cook.

"Hmmm," said Soda Pop. "I'm only a good cook when I can gobble up everything I make. As long as I can do that, whatever I make is delicious!"

"But you'd be cooking it for me," said the pot-bellied man.

"Oh no, I'm afraid that wouldn't work," Soda Pop said gloomily.

So they moved on again.

Soon they came across a little church with a gold cross on top. The giraffe went for a nap in the churchyard because he wasn't allowed in.

Just inside the door they found a clergyman.

"Good day to you. I'm looking for a job," said Soda Pop.

"What can you do, my child?" asked the clergyman.

"I can shoot things and fight with army knives," said Mazarin.

But the clergyman had been asking Soda Pop.

"I can do almost anything in the world," said Soda Pop, "except peel potatoes or cook meals."

"Can you take the collection and put up the hymn numbers on Sundays?"

Soda Pop had to stop and think. "Which numbers would I have to put up?"

"They'd be different every time," said the clergyman.

"All right, as long as I don't have to put up any threes, because I always get them upside down," said Soda Pop. But taking the collection sounded great. "Can I keep it all myself?" he asked.

"Certainly not. It's for the poor," said the clergyman. And after that he decided against the idea of giving Soda Pop a job at the church. "Farewell, farewell," he said, closing the door.

They rode home on the giraffe, but at the hotdoggery they climbed off and went in.

"Oh, it's you again," said the hotdog man.

"Yes, it's us, and we need a thousand hotdogs, quick as you can," said Soda Pop.

"Do you have the money now, then?"

"No, money is one thing we don't have." Soda Pop tilted his head. "But maybe we can do a swap. We'll give you a tiger in exchange for the hotdogs."

The hotdog man looked startled.

"A live tiger?"

"A real live tiger, large as life and twice as lethal," said Soda Pop.

The hotdog man had a good think about it and gave his hotdogs a sad look.

"Come and fetch it whenever you like," said Soda Pop. "All you have to do is yank open the barn door and grab one."

Then Soda Pop and Mazarin snatched up all the hotdogs they could see, leapt onto the giraffe, and galloped home.

The nearer they got, the louder the growls from the barn grew. It was a terrible racket.

"Uh-oh, they're so ravenous I daren't open the door," said Soda Pop. "You do it, Mazarin."

"No fear, let's get Dartanyong to do it," said Mazarin.

So they went and knocked at Dartanyong's door. His head buzz was so loud you could hear it right out by the block where they chopped the firewood. He was sitting in bed in his winter coat and leather cap, putting marks on a chart.

"You're as fit as a fiddle, I see," roared Soda Pop.

Dartanyong started up like a rocket.

"No, no, my temperature's so high the thermometer broke in half. I have a bout of appendicitis too," moaned Dartanyong.

"You could still toss the tigers a few hotdogs, couldn't you?" said Soda Pop.

At first Dartanyong couldn't hear what he was saying. It took a minute to realize that Soda Pop was talking about the tigers, but then he perked up and jumped out of bed.

He was limping very badly.

"What's this, is your appendix in your leg, man?" said Soda Pop.

It wasn't, of course, but he'd put his leg in a sling in case he took a tumble.

So Dartanyong limped out, leaning on Mazarin and Soda Pop, and they hid round the corner while he opened the barn door and handed out hotdogs right and left and scratched a few tigers behind the ears. Then he closed the door quietly and discreetly.

"If anyone asks for me, I'll be in the woodshed compiling hotdog charts. Good night," he said.

Soda Pop and Mazarin went into the kitchen. Soda Pop was pleased with his day. He was particularly pleased that he hadn't been able to find a job.

"Heaven and pancakes, what a relief not to have to work!" he yelled, flitting around the room like a butterfly.

The Championship

One morning, Soda Pop and Mazarin strolled around taking a look at their house. It was a good house and had little turrets here and there, with brass knobs on them. It had shutters too, some with windows and some without. None of them could be opened or closed because Soda Pop had nailed them shut for security.

"Well, a small balcony wouldn't hurt," muttered Soda Pop. "And a couple more turrets wouldn't do any harm either. But what we need most of all," he said, staring dreamily across the lawn, "are a few running tracks and somewhere to pole vault and that sort of thing, so we can hold competitions. Do you think Dartanyong's got a stopwatch?"

Mazarin was dead certain Dartanyong had at least ten, fanatical as he was about times and charts. They knocked on the door of the woodshed and found Dartanyong in bed, terribly ill as usual. He had such a buzzing in his ears that he'd forgotten his own name, he said.

"So what *is* your name then?" asked Soda Pop.

"I don't know, something beginning with D," Dartanyong whined.

He had stopwatches, anyway, loads of them, so they took a few and went back into the garden.

Then they zoomed round and round with the lawnmower until they'd made a proper track. They wrote FINISH on a big piece of paper so they'd know who'd won.

Then Soda Pop set up a pole-vault bar using an old pair of Dartanyong's skis.

"We ought to have a go-kart track as well," said Soda Pop, "and make a go-kart out of old lawnmowers. But let's leave that for another day. We need a football field as well. And an ice-hockey rink. Get to work!"

They were hard at it for several hours. The ice-hockey rink looked splendid, with little fences around it and a couple of old carrier bags as goals.

"I know, let's compete against the tigers and see who wins," said Soda Pop. "I'm not bringing them out, though!" he added quickly, because the tigers were growling like crazy in the barn.

They went to fetch Dartanyong, who was feeling a bit better and could almost remember his name and that he was Soda Pop's pop.

"You can time us, then compile nice big charts and tables with minutes and seconds and so on," said Soda Pop. He squeezed Dartanyong into an old sugar crate, so he could be the track referee.

"Ready, steady, go!" Dartanyong called.

Soda Pop and Mazarin shot off like rockets around the track. Mazarin led the whole way and crossed the finishing line several lengths ahead of Soda Pop.

"Mazarin won in fourteen seconds flat!" yelled Dartanyong, looking at his stopwatch.

"Oh, come off it, that must be a mistake," said Soda Pop. "Let's re-run it."

So they re-ran it and Mazarin won the second race, too, by even more than the first.

"No, something's gone wrong again." Soda Pop shook his head. "I have to win, because I'm better."

So they ran five more races, with Dartanyong compiling a big chart, and Mazarin won every single time.

"We'll have a game of ice hockey instead," decided Soda Pop. "Dartanyong can be goalie. I'm Russia and Mazarin's Canada, same as usual. Mazarin, fetch the brooms and let's get started!"

Mazarin came back with the brooms and away they went, with a green tomato as a puck.

Soda Pop was as happy as a lark; he was very good at ice hockey. He scored eleven goals in ten minutes and Dartanyong was so busy writing them all down, he didn't have time to defend the goal.

Mazarin was quickly bored with ice hockey, so he squatted in his goal and ate the puck.

"Well, I've got a cracking lead in this championship," said Soda Pop smugly. "Shall we let the tigers play now?"

But they weren't keen on the idea. The tigers were still growling so loudly that the whole barn was one big rumble.

"If they weren't so deadly dangerous, I'd go and get them this instant," said Soda Pop. He swept Dartanyong's feet from under him so he hit the ground like a felled pine tree.

"Are you crazy?" sputtered Dartanyong, struggling to his feet.

"Phooey, I was only getting in a bit of training. You know, boxing. Don't you recognize a joke when one hits you?"

Then it was time for the pole vault and the going got tough. They both cleared forty centimetres. And then they cleared fifty. And sixty.

Then they had to finish because the old skis collapsed and Dartanyong broke the point of his pencil.

Soda Pop sat on the front steps and sang, "As long as you keep on loving, you stay young..." until Dartanyong had sharpened his pencil and it was time for more events.

They ran the sprint and, strangely, Soda Pop won, even though he came last. Then they swam a full length butterfly in the swimming pool and they both won, which was pretty good considering neither of them could swim.

They each had so many points by now that Dartanyong had no more room on his charts.

"You can keep your own scores now," he said, stumping off to the woodshed.

"That's enough competition. Let's award points for other things instead," said Soda Pop. "A blackbird, for instance, is worth one point. An owl's worth ten points, and a tiger a thousand points, if you get what I mean."

Mazarin didn't get it at all, but he wanted to play anyway.

"I can see a sparrow!" he shouted. "There in the birch tree!"

"Ah well, that's minus five points," Soda Pop told him. "But there's a woodpecker, seven points, and a dead bumblebee, three points."

"I see a grasshopper and a great big fly," said Mazarin.

"No points for those, I'm afraid," said Soda Pop. "They're beyond the cut-off."

Then Soda Pop saw a broken jug and some big blue flowers, and his points came pouring in.

"I see a sunflower and a rusty hammer," said Mazarin.

"One point, almost," said Soda Pop.

Then they felt thirsty and went in for a drink of fruit fizz.

Soda Pop got points for every gulp he took, but Mazarin only got a few when he dropped his glass on the floor.

Soda Pop was sitting at the table looking out of the window, and suddenly he stiffened.

"Quiet, I think that was an elk running past, shhh," he said. "No, it was only a blackbird. Two points, always worth having!"

When they tallied up their points they found that Soda Pop had five hundred and sixty-eight and Mazarin had seven.

"But if you rustle up some chocolate pudding with whipped cream, you'll get an extra five hundred and sixty-one points and then we'll both be champions. Congratulations!" yelled Soda Pop.

The Cushiest Jail
in the World

One morning, Dartanyong came knocking at Soda Pop's door. He had a gigantic monkey wrench under his arm.

Soda Pop and Mazarin jumped up from the floor where they'd been sleeping. They were surprised because Dartanyong didn't knock at their door unless it was something very important.

"Good day, are there any broken pipes that need fixing?" squeaked Dartanyong.

"No, there aren't, and what's got into you?" said Soda Pop.

"I'm a plumber. Good day to you, and I'm looking for pipes that need fixing," Dartanyong said again. He slammed the monkey wrench down on the draining board and made the whole house jump.

"So you've turned to plumbing in your old age?" asked Soda Pop in astonishment.

"Whaddya mean? I've been a plumber all my life," said Dartanyong. He could hear perfectly. His ear buzz had gone for the time being.

"How funny, he thinks he's a plumber," whispered Mazarin. "Go on, let him fix a few pipes."

They really didn't have any broken pipes, but Soda Pop thought it hardly mattered.

"If he carries on lashing out like that they soon will be broken," he said.

So they let Dartanyong loose on the biggest pipe in the house. Dartanyong started hammering and bashing, and soon the pipe

was in smithereens that tinkled onto the floor. A fountain of water spurted from the wall.

"Right, all done," said Dartanyong with satisfaction. "That'll be forty-nine seventy-five. The bill will be in the mail. Good afternoon." Swinging his monkey wrench, he tootled off back to the woodshed.

"How weird that Dartanyong thought he was a plumber," said Mazarin. "Maybe tomorrow he'll think he's a carpenter."

"I like having a fountain in the kitchen," said Soda Pop, showering off his dusty old bathrobe.

After breakfast they sneaked about to hear how peeved the tigers were. But all they heard from the barn was snoring.

"Just as well, because Dartanyong won't dare go in there today if he thinks he's a plumber," said Soda Pop.

Then they heard a noise behind the garage and the next moment the cross old man popped out. Following him was a policeman with a sword dangling from his belt.

"Yes, here they are," the cross old man told the policeman. "They own the owls that are living in my mailbox. They're all round the bend here, if you ask me. They've got a giraffe on their rubbish heap, to boot."

The policeman took out his notebook and started to write: *Red owls. Two of them in a yellow mailbox.* And then he wrote that they might all be round the bend.

"Now everybody, come along to the mailbox, please," he said, twitching his sword.

They all marched off to the cross old man's mailbox.

42

He banged the lid open. It was empty except for a letter from a school friend he'd forgotten.

The policeman took out his notebook and wrote: *Mailbox empty*.

"But they were in there this morning, snoring," said the cross old man. "Red monsters with puffed-up bellies."

The policeman sighed. "All right, what shall we do now?" he said, putting away his notebook.

"Put them in jail, of course," said the cross old man. "And there's no roof on their garage, you know. They've turned it into a swimming pool."

"Some folk think they're plumbers and others like throwing people into jail," said Soda Pop peaceably. "Me, I like playing pop music at dawn. But I don't mind coming along to jail because I've heard it's extra nice there."

"It's a very pleasant little jail." The policeman tied their hands with rope before they set off.

The cross old man came along, too, to make sure it was all done properly.

They soon came to a forest and in the middle was a little jailhouse with a hammock outside. The jailhouse was red with white corners and a little robber looking out of every window.

A few more were relaxing in the hammock, smoking chocolate cigarettes. Soda Pop said hello and gave polite bows to right and left. This was the place for him, he could feel it.

The policeman opened the door and let them into the jailhouse. It was time for his coffee, which was bubbling away in

the kitchen. Another policeman took over, a right little rascal. He cut the ropes off their wrists and fished a notebook out of *his* pocket.

"If you've ever been bitten by a red owl, where did it bite you?" he asked, glaring at the cross old man.

"On my big toe, but why do you ask?" The cross old man waggled his ears.

The policeman shook his head as he busily wrote things in his notebook and rubbed them out. "What's your name?"

"Soda Pop," said Soda Pop.

"That's not a name, it's a soft drink. What's your real name?"

"Well, sorry, but my name really is Soda Pop," said Soda Pop.

"And is it true that you're in the habit of lying under the kitchen table, cracking nuts?" The policeman's pencil scratched noisily at the paper.

"Yep, that's exactly what I do," Soda Pop said happily.

"And you have a giraffe that eats beds?"

Soda Pop nodded.

"Of course, you don't have a job?" said the policeman, writing like mad.

"No, of course I don't," Soda Pop agreed.

The policeman looked thoughtful. "Next one," he said.

"But I haven't done a thing," said Mazarin. "I'm too little. I've no idea about anything."

"Do you and your dad often play ice hockey with old brooms?" asked the policeman.

"Yes, we do. I'm Canada and Soda Pop is Russia," said Mazarin.

"What was the score last time?"

"Five–nil to Russia," said Mazarin, disgruntled.

"You play a lot with army knives, I suppose," said the policeman.

"Yes, every day," said Mazarin. "But if things get too danger-ous I start shooting instead."

The policeman closed his eyes and put down his notebook.

"Listen, I'm here to report red owls making themselves at home in my mailbox," said the cross old man nervously.

"I can't be expected to bother with that," said the policeman. "There's no law against sleeping in mailboxes. Let them snore as much as they like!"

The policeman looked at his watch and saw it was time for his coffee, too.

"Gentlemen," he said, "I'm afraid there's no room for you in our jail. The fact is, we can't take in just anybody and you lot seem as mad as hatters. You'd better go home. Good afternoon."

And he nipped away before his Danish pastries went cold. Soda Pop, Mazarin, and the cross old man went out through the front door of the jail. Everyone was happy except Soda Pop, who would have liked to stay a month or two and look around.

On the steps they met a robber who seemed very nice.

"Wouldn't they let you stay?" he asked.

Soda Pop shook his head gloomily.

"No, they don't take just anybody here," said the robber, swelling with importance. "And nobody's going to be let into any sort of jail with a hat like that on their noggin."

Soda Pop felt his head with his hands and realized he was wearing his old tea cosy, the big one with the blue flowery pattern.

"I thought I was unusually hot about the ears today," he said. "My name's Soda Pop, by the way. Do come and visit some time. I live over that way!"

"I'm Gustav. I'll come on Sunday at quarter past two on the dot," said the robber.

It was evening by the time they reached home. Dartanyong was sitting outside the woodshed quivering like an aspen leaf because the tigers were growling like crazy.

"Ooh, it's horrible," he wailed. "I was just quietly sitting there, compiling a chart of pipes to mend, but I couldn't go on. My dear friends, what's all this growling?"

"Come off it, Dartanyong, it's only the tigers. You remember them, don't you?" snapped Soda Pop. "You a retired tiger tamer and all."

"Me, no, I've been a plumber all my life." Dartanyong brandished his monkey wrench.

Soda Pop gave a sigh.

"We'll talk to him tomorrow instead," he said to Mazarin. "He might have forgotten all this plumbo jumbo by then."

"Yes, because who the dickens is going to feed the tigers if Dartanyong daren't?" said Mazarin.

They left Dartanyong and threw themselves into the swimming pool for a bit.

Mazarin clean forgot that he couldn't swim, so he only managed a couple of quick, foamy circuits before he sank to the bottom.

The car was so dirty by now you could hardly see it and the pike were squeaking about between the floor pedals.

"What shall we give the tigers to eat?" Soda Pop asked through bubbles.

"Hotdogs," said Mazarin.

"You said it!"

They splashed their way up and Soda Pop wrung cascades of water from the tea cosy.

The giraffe stood dozing on the rubbish heap, so all they had to do was leap aboard, and off they went. It was dark when they reached the hotdoggery and the hotdog man had gone home.

Soda Pop opened the door and started shovelling hotdogs into a big bag.

"We haven't got any money, though," said Mazarin.

So Soda Pop found a piece of paper and a pen and wrote: *We came for som hottox so now yoo can have anuther tiger. Thats nice for yoo. Best wizhes Soda Pop*

He left the note on the counter. Then they lugged out all the hotdogs.

"With a bit of luck I could go to jail for this. I mean, I'm almost a robber," said Soda Pop as they galloped home.

But standing outside the barn with the hotdogs, they could hear the tigers kicking up a terrible growly fuss. Neither Soda Pop nor Mazarin dared to open the door.

"Let's try Dartanyong again. Maybe he's over the plumbing," said Soda Pop.

They knocked at the woodshed door and Soda Pop called out, "Is the plumber at home?"

"Yes," piped Dartanyong.

"Never mind, it doesn't matter," said Soda Pop and they left the bag of hotdogs outside the barn and went indoors.

Soda Pop and Mazarin lay down on the floor in the reddest room where Soda Pop had switched on a few lamps to make it cosy. Before he nodded off he pulled the tea cosy right down over his ears.

"I've never had such a lovely hat, before or since," he said. "Whoever wakes up first has to feed the tigers. Good night."

And he fell fast asleep.

Mister Dartanyong,
Famous Flying Trapeze Artist

Mazarin was first to wake the next morning.

Soda Pop would never have dreamt of waking up first. For the life of him, he didn't dare feed the tigers.

Once Mazarin had managed to shove open the front door, a wave of growls washed over him. The air vibrated with them.

Almost at once, Dartanyong came cantering over in spangled trunks and with sequins in his hair.

"Morning, Mister Plumber!" shouted Mazarin.

"Plumber," sputtered Dartanyong. "I'm no plumber. I'm a famous flying trapeze artist." And he hung by one elbow from the drainpipe until it came crashing to the ground.

"Great, if you're a famous flying trapeze artist, you won't mind chucking the tigers a few hotdogs," said Mazarin.

"Not at all." Dartanyong charged over to the barn with a whoop, yanked open the door and threw the bag of hotdogs straight at the heap of tigers. Then he carefully closed the door and hitched up his swimming trunks, which had fallen down with the speed of it all.

Little Dartanyong made a wonderful trapeze artist: bendy as a bait worm and thin as a rake. The moment the tigers went quiet, Soda Pop woke and jumped up to look out of the nearest window. Seeing Dartanyong, he went into fits of laughter and had to lie down for a few minutes before he went out onto the front steps.

"Good morning, Mister Plumber!" he yelled. "Thanks for helping with the hotdogs!"

"Plumber, my foot," said Dartanyong sulkily. "I don't know why you keep calling me a plumber."

"It's the famous flying trapeze artist, can't you see?" said Mazarin.

Another gale of laughter almost knocked Soda Pop out again, but he bucked up and came outside to feel Dartanyong's muscles.

"Not bad. Almost as big as walnuts," he said.

Dartanyong was very impressed with Soda Pop's tea cosy. "Amazing hat you've got there," he said. "I've never seen anything like it."

"It's a good hat." Soda Pop pulled it down over his ears. "A touch too warm in a heat wave, perhaps. Why not come in and have a seat, though it's nothing special."

Dartanyong remained on his feet. He was more used to the circus, he explained.

In the end, they all went in, and as Dartanyong stepped through the door he felt the urge to swing from the trapeze, so Mazarin dug out some old skipping ropes, which they attached here and there to the ceiling. Then Dartanyong threw himself from one room to the next; the red one in particular felt just like the Big Top, he said. He was so enthusiastic that the elastic came out of his spangled trunks and they eventually flopped to the floor.

Dartanyong clung to the ceiling light.

"Mend my trunks!" he cried. "The elastic's gone!"

Soda Pop and Mazarin hunted through all their drawers and cupboards. Finally they found a reel of thread and a rascally little needle, sharp as sharp, under the kitchen table.

Soda Pop sewed giant criss-cross stitches all over the trunks, while Dartanyong froze his bum off, up there on the ceiling light.

Soda Pop groaned as the needle kept pricking him, but at last the trunks were ready. There wasn't room to thread the elastic back in because he'd sewed too close to the top, but Dartanyong didn't notice since he put them on upside down, with one leg round his tummy.

"They're a good snug fit now," he said, "though one leg seems to be flapping about!"

"All the better for flying on that trapeze," said Soda Pop.

Then Soda Pop and Mazarin wanted to join the circus act. They sprinkled sequins in their hair and started whooping too.

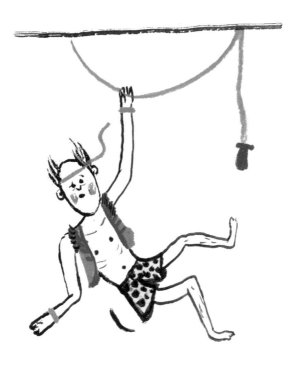

But Mazarin was unlucky. In the black room, he flew straight into a wall. He had funny tunes playing in his head for a long time after that. In the end they piped down and there was only a faint ringing, deep inside. He opened his eyes to find he was lying on the floor, staring.

Soda Pop was sitting beside him, white as a sheet.

"Are you dead, Mazarin?" he whispered.

"No, I'm not dead." Mazarin sat up. "But there's a telliphone ringing in the middle of my head."

Soda Pop listened hard.

"You're right," he said, "there's a telliphone ringing!"

And he dashed off to the green room and lifted the receiver.

It was the cross old man.

"I just wanted to let you know I'll be round in a little while for coffee. Goodbye," he said, and hung up.

"Goodbye." Soda Pop went to put the coffee pot on the stove.

While the coffee was coming to the boil they charged around with bendy sticks in their mouths, pretending to be rhinoceroses.

Three and a half hours later, the cross old man turned up, tired and out of puff.

"How's things, apart from that?" asked Soda Pop.

"Well, my mailbox was stuffed with owls this morning," said the cross old man. "Things will come to a crunch soon, you wait and see!"

Soda Pop, singing to himself, tossed the sugar lumps and cups onto the table. "Coffee's up!" he bawled, pouring some.

Dartanyong came bouncing into the kitchen. The cross old man stared, wide-eyed.

"What's this supposed to be?" he said. "Is it a worm or a man? And what the heck are those old pants he's wearing!"

Dartanyong was terribly insulted and sat at the far end of the kitchen, saying nothing.

"This is my father, the famous trapeze artist. We're pleased to meet you," said Soda Pop with a bow.

"Good gracious me," said the cross old man, looking away.

Then he took a big gulp of his coffee.

A second later he sprayed it all over the table and started coughing and leaping around.

"What foul coffee!" he yelled. "It's black as pitch, look at it! Pitch-black coffee just kills me."

So Soda Pop made him a whole pot of wishy-washy coffee and the cross old man downed twelve cups, one after another, until his tummy was slopping and gurgling like the sea.

While they had their coffee, Dartanyong dozed off in his corner. He wasn't used to all this hanging and swinging, so he was pretty worn out.

Then there was a tremendous racket from the yard. It was the giraffe, back from the forest. A bit of bedspread stuck out of the corner of his mouth so he'd probably stolen someone's bed again.

The cross old man took a long look at the bit of bedspread.

"It's the hotdog man's," he said.

At that very moment there was a crunching on the gravel and the hotdog man came running up, all out of puff.

"He's eaten my best bed, that blasted giraffe," he sobbed, "and my Persian bedspread and the mattress Great-grandfather slept on."

He cried floods of tears that streamed onto the kitchen table. And when he'd finished crying about his bed, he couldn't stop but had a good cry about the fact that all his hotdogs were gone as well, and that his mother was cross with him once when he was small.

Soda Pop did his best to comfort the hotdog man and kept offering him wishy-washy coffee and pitch-black coffee while Mazarin dried his tears with a big bath towel.

"I've got no bed and no hotdogs," sobbed the hotdog man.

"But you have two tigers," said Soda Pop, tickling him under the chin. "And here's some money for sweets."

Remembering the tigers, the hotdog man stopped crying and stuffed the money into his pocket.

"Yes, you can pick out a couple," said Soda Pop. "Pull the barn door open smartish and catch them as they run by. It's easy peasy!"

"But they can be dangerous. You'll have to help me," said the hotdog man.

"Not on your life," said Soda Pop. "But the famous flying trapeze artist here will help you, I'm sure."

And he shoved Dartanyong and the hotdog man out of the door and slammed it shut behind them.

He and Mazarin lay low and kept an eye out of the window as Dartanyong and the hotdog man shuffled across the yard.

Dartanyong fiddled with the key in the lock and with a metallic screech the door finally opened. They both disappeared into the total darkness.

They were gone so long that even Soda Pop got nervous and started thinking about the grave under the oak where the violets grew in spring.

"You'll have to do the watering on Mondays and I'll take Thursdays," he told Mazarin.

"What are you talking about? We never do any watering, do we?" said Mazarin.

"The flowers on Dartanyong's grave."

At that moment the barn door flew open and out came the hotdog man with his hotdog cycle cart. In the cart two tigers lay fast asleep and snoring, and perched on top of them, bright as a button, with feathers fluttering around his ears, was Dartanyong.

Then Soda Pop and Mazarin felt safe enough to go outside again. Soda Pop was glad he wouldn't have to go and do the watering on Thursdays. He hated watering.

Dartanyong went back into his woodshed but the hotdog man stood for a long time, patting the tigers.

"Well, heaven preserve you when they wake up all hungry," said Soda Pop. "Good luck, good luck." He started waving to hurry the hotdog man on his way. "And if they won't do what they're told, bite their tails! Cheery bye."

Gustav the Robber Drops By

On Sunday at quarter past two, Gustav the robber came bouncing along the road. He'd been given time off from jail and here he was.

Soda Pop thought they should take a little dip first, because the weather was glorious. They climbed up onto the garage and Gustav was very taken with the pool when he saw the water and heard the pikes squeaking. He quickly threw off his clothes and stood there in nothing but his undiepants. They were his best ones, as it happened, with a fish pattern of perch. Mazarin's eyes nearly popped out of his head when he saw that Gustav's whole body was covered in tattoos. On his tummy were big hearts and sea serpents and naked ladies, and sailing across his chest was a full-rigged galleon.

"How did you get so swanky?" asked Mazarin.

"I drew all over myself with a ballpoint pen," said Gustav.

Soda Pop, too, was mightily impressed and he felt a bit embarrassed taking off his bathrobe when he didn't have a single picture on his body.

"We'll go inside and draw on ourselves after our swim," he announced.

So they dived in head first, all three. Soda Pop kept his tea cosy hat on, so he wouldn't get water in his ears.

Once they'd finished diving they floated on their backs and chatted about this and that. Soda Pop told Gustav about the tigers, the giraffe and the owls and Gustav thought he'd come to a really nice place.

Eventually they sloshed out onto the side of the pool. Gustav was disgruntled because his tattoos had faded in the water.

"Let's go in and touch them up with my ballpoint pen," suggested Soda Pop.

They sat in a row on the kitchen bench and Gustav carefully filled in all his hearts and sea serpents until they were a deep, dark blue once more.

"There, I feel human again," he said. "Now let's get drawing on you two."

He covered Mazarin and Soda Pop in serpents and anchors, and in the middle of Mazarin's tummy he drew a large lady without a stitch of clothing.

"Now you're starting to look a bit more civilized," Gustav said happily.

Once their tattoos were finished, they went out and strutted about the yard. Mazarin was curious to know who Dartanyong was being today. He hadn't seen hide or hair of him since the evening before.

"Mister trapeze artist, are you there?" called Soda Pop, whacking the woodshed with a big stick.

"Hello, who is it?" came a weedy little voice.

They wrenched open the door and stormed in.

Dartanyong was lying in bed, all pale and white.

"How's things, famous flying trapeze artist?" yelled Soda Pop.

"Flying trapeze artist, why call me that?" piped Dartanyong. "Have you forgotten your own father's name?"

"Oh, is it really you, Dartanyong?"

"Who else would it be?" said Dartanyong.

"Ah, all right." Soda Pop was disappointed. "In that case, this is Dartanyong, my dad. And this is Gustav from the jailhouse, where he's a robber. Say hello nicely now."

"Hello," said Gustav. "How's things?"

"Not good, not good at all," whimpered Dartanyong. "I had a temperature that took up half the thermometer this morning, and one of my legs is dangling loose as if it might come off...I sneezed three times in a row at twenty-five past seven. And my ears are buzzing so I can't find my charts."

Gustav looked a bit perplexed.

"We've just drawn all over ourselves," said Soda Pop. "Would you like Gustav to draw on you, too?"

"Not on your life. Don't come so close, either, or the germs will jump across and get me," said Dartanyong.

Gustav went around looking at Dartanyong's collection of cups and prizes. He'd won prizes for triple jump and pole vault and had even managed to get one for butterfly stroke. Gustav was most interested in a shelf of silver cups with special marks stamped on the bottom.

"Yes, they're very fine mugs," piped Dartanyong. "They're worth a fortune, though I got them cheap of course."

Then they had to go, because Dartanyong got the shakes in his toes and the whole woodshed started quaking.

Mazarin thought Gustav looked different from before. He had two huge lumps on his tummy.

"How did you get those?" he asked.

"Oh, they're just insect bites," said Gustav. "They'll have gone down by tonight."

Even Soda Pop thought they were unusually big for insect bites, but if that's what they were then it was okay.

They played football for a while with old cucumbers Mazarin found behind the garage, but Gustav was so good at it that they soon gave up.

"Let's play cops and robbers now. It's great fun and the only game I'm really decent at," said Gustav.

"Who's going to be the robber then?" asked Mazarin.

"Who do you think, nitwit!" said Gustav. "You'll have to be the cops. And I need a five-minute head start. When I shout 'Ready!' you can come after me."

Gustav made himself scarce while Soda Pop and Mazarin lurked behind the woodshed.

After what seemed like forever there was a shout of "Ready!" from inside their house. They ran in and started searching all the rooms. He wasn't in the kitchen or in the green room. But the coffee pots had gone and all the glasses and Soda Pop's telliphone books. The telliphone was missing too, and Mazarin's best swimming trunks and all the lamps and brass knobs.

They dashed into the blue room, then the red room where loads more stuff was missing. The sofa was still in place, and the tables.

But the loose change usually lying about under the drawers had gone and so had the radio.

"He really is an expert dab hand at this game, that Gustav," said Soda Pop.

They searched and searched and turned everything upside down, but they didn't find Gustav.

In the end he got fed up and came out of his own accord.

"Where have you hidden it all, man?" asked Soda Pop.

"Where have I hidden it?" yelled Gustav. "Are we playing cops and robbers or not? Get out there and hunt for it!"

Soda Pop and Mazarin hunted and hunted; they hunted everywhere, but they couldn't find anything.

Meanwhile, Gustav sneaked off again, and when Soda Pop and Mazarin had finished their hunt, and went back inside, the sofas and tables were gone. And the rugs and all the withered old houseplants. It was incredible how empty the place was!

"That's what happens when you play cops and robbers!" laughed Gustav. "Out you go and keep on looking, or I'll keep the lot."

While Soda Pop and Mazarin looked, Gustav followed them around, tittering and thinking how stupid they were.

"Think about it," he said. "They're not in the woodshed or on the rubbish heap. Not in the swimming pool or the scrap shed. Not in the main house or the henhouse. So where are they?"

Mazarin and Soda Pop racked their brains but they couldn't think of anywhere else.

"If you say 'in the barn' you won't be wrong," Gustav prompted them at last.

"In the barn!" chorused Soda Pop and Mazarin, wide-eyed. "Didn't they gobble you up?"

"No worse than usual," said Gustav.

"But didn't they look horribly angry?" said Soda Pop.

"Phooey, it was black as pitch in there. I couldn't see a thing. I just chucked in the lamps, sofas and glasses. It was dead easy!"

"Well, I'm not going to fetch them all back," said Soda Pop.

"Nor me," said Mazarin.

"Nor me, because I'm the robber in this game, after all," said Gustav.

They had to go and get Dartanyong even though his leg was a bit loose and wonky. Dartanyong flapped like an extractor fan in and out of the barn with sofas and lamps and brass knobs. After several hours he was finally reaching the end.

Then Gustav looked at his watch. "Lads, I've got to get back," he said. "It was fun while it lasted. Next time I'll hide even more of your stuff."

"Gosh, look how your insect bites have swollen!" said Mazarin.

"Yes, they've come on pretty well." Gustav gave them a gentle squeeze. "I expect they'll pop tonight! Cheerio. See you when I see you."

Soda Pop and Mazarin were worn out after Gustav left. Not to mention Dartanyong, who was totally exhausted.

Soda Pop and Mazarin fell asleep on the grass, while Dartanyong limped into the woodshed to go to bed. But he came tearing straight out again.

"Hey, my best silver mugs are gone! Gustav must have stolen them!" He wrung his skinny hands. "My best silver mugs that I bought so cheap!"

Soda Pop thought hard for a moment.

"The insect bites," he said.

"No, not insect bites, I said silver mugs," moaned Dartanyong.

"It must be the bites." Soda Pop and Mazarin nodded at one another.

"I'll give you some really nice plastic mugs if you just stop whining," Soda Pop told Dartanyong.

A bit later, Soda Pop realized that his best brass knobs were gone, and all the money under the stove.

"No wonder they were so huge, those bites," he sighed. He fetched the telliphone and called the jail.

"Er, Gustav," he said, "did you happen to take anything with you from here by mistake?"

"Yes, weirdly enough, I found I'd brought home loads of things without meaning to," said Gustav. "Those insect bites were chock-full! Shall I bring them all back?"

"It's okay, you can keep them. We have too much clutter anyway. But if you'd put the brass knobs in an envelope and send them back, they were my best ones. Cheery bye," said Soda Pop, hanging up.

A Gold Toilet
for Soda Pop

Next morning, Soda Pop and Mazarin woke at exactly the same time. They'd had exactly the same dream, too. But they'd both forgotten what it was, because we forget our dreams almost at once. Then they had yogurt brimming over with crunchy flakes and drifts of sugar. Soda Pop turned on some pop music and sang "Come to me and kiss me slowly, gently, lovely," spraying oat puffs in all directions.

At ten past nine a horn honked outside on the road. It was the mail van.

"My turn to wrestle the delivery man to the ground!" yelled Soda Pop. He wound his bathrobe around his stomach a few times and trotted off.

He and Mazarin took it in turns to wrestle the postman to the ground. You see, the postman was so protective of his letters, it was the only way to get them off him.

While he was waiting for his turn, Mazarin went out to the rubbish heap and scratched the giraffe. Its eyes were starting to glaze over, which probably meant it was heading for another bed-eating phase.

Soda Pop was soon back. He hadn't managed to get his hands on any letters, of course, and he'd dropped the newspaper in a waterhole on the way back.

"Let's go and see how Dartanyong is today," he said.

They had to knock for quite a while before Dartanyong opened the door. He was wearing old work clothes and an empty paper bag on his head.

"Do I have the pleasure of addressing Dartanyong?" asked Soda Pop.

"Absolutely not," said Dartanyong.

"Who are you, then?"

"The name's Pettersson, master painter Pettersson. Just say the word and I'll come and repaint everything for you," said Dartanyong.

Soda Pop said the word at once and Dartanyong grabbed up assorted buckets of paint and brushes and came along with him.

"Please have a seat while I think about how we want it to look," said Soda Pop when they got inside.

Dartanyong went into the red room while he waited and pried off a few lids and that sort of thing.

When Soda Pop had finished thinking and came in, it was no

longer a red room but a yellow one. Dartanyong had painted the sofa and curtains too, because they were in the way, he said.

"So how much does this cost?" asked Soda Pop.

"Ten will do it," said Dartanyong. "The bill will come by mail."

Then Dartanyong painted the green room pale blue, and the kitchen mauve. But he made the bathroom so grand that Soda Pop almost jumped out of his trousers. He'd painted the floor, walls and ceiling in pure, solid gold: the whole bathroom, including the pipes.

"I'm going to move in here forever," cried Soda Pop. He dashed off to fetch the drawer where he kept his clothes and undiepants, books, photos and brass knobs, and started to furnish the place.

"Just remember one thing," he told Mazarin sternly. "From today there's to be no more rushing to the toilet for us. You can't treat a gold toilet just any old how!"

"But what if I badly need to go?" asked Mazarin.

"You'll have to get over it," said Soda Pop cheerily. "With a bit of willpower, most things in this world are possible!"

Dartanyong whistled under his breath as he stumbled through the house with the paint flowing in a steady stream. Soon every room had been repainted. Then he took the paper bag off his head and wrote out a bill.

Painting of one room, he wrote. *And another. And another. And another. And another. And a bathroom. And another room. 1000 exactly.*

Then Dartanyong trudged home to his woodshed, got into bed and went to sleep.

As for Soda Pop, he went into his bathroom and polished brass knobs and thought life was wonderful.

Fifteen minutes later, the hotdog man came rushing up, bright red in the face. Tired and cross, he flung himself down in the yard.

His tigers had run away in the night, he said. They gave a few growls, then ran off, goodness knows where. There wasn't a single trace of them.

Dartanyong came out of the woodshed and introduced himself very thoroughly.

"Gorgeous weather," he said. "It makes you want to paint and dance."

He hooked down a can of gold paint from the roof and painted bits of the hotdog man, who was completely baffled. He scarcely recognized Dartanyong with the enormous paper bag on his head.

"But aren't you Mister Dartanyong, Soda Pop's father?" he kept saying, shaking himself so he was surrounded by a cloud of gold.

"Master painter Pettersson, if you don't mind." Dartanyong bowed until he felt quite dizzy.

The hotdog man stared at Dartanyong in fascination and forgot all about his escaped tigers and how furious he was.

Dartanyong painted the hotdog man's trousers from the ankles up. Then he sloshed a bit of paint on his shoulders and ears.

Meanwhile, Mazarin came sauntering along. He felt a little bit sorry for the hotdog man, being painted all over like that.

"Why not go and paint a few tigers in the barn instead?" he joked.

Dartanyong was off like a shot!

Mazarin was scared stiff so he dashed in to Soda Pop.

"Dartanyong will be gobbled up; he's trying to paint the tigers!" he yelled.

"Oh, I'll watch through the kitchen window," said Soda Pop, cheering up no end.

First Dartanyong painted the barn door, then the doorstep, then he opened the door and painted a few tigers as they charged past.

"Any minute now there'll be nothing left of Dartanyong but the paper bag." Soda Pop pressed his nose to the windowpane.

But Dartanyong got away with it this time, too, and emerged with an empty paint can, whistling in satisfaction.

"Twenty gold tigers! The bill will be in the mail," he shouted.

"Come to me and kiss me slowly, gently, lovely," sang Soda Pop, coming out onto the front steps with the tea cosy hat pulled well down over his head.

"Not on your Nelly," sniffed Dartanyong.

But Soda Pop went into such a fit of giggles that he fell over, and the hotdog man howled with laughter.

Once they had calmed down, they agreed that the hotdog man could pick out a couple more tigers. If they ran away as well he

could come back for two more, if he dared. It didn't matter a bit because, as Soda Pop said, the barn was stuffed with tigers.

He invited the hotdog man and Dartanyong into the bathroom for a while, and it was unimaginably fancy with all that floor-to-ceiling gold. The hotdog man took a seat on the sink and Dartanyong on the toilet, then they ate a bit of toothpaste that Soda Pop found in the bathroom cabinet. They were having a really nice time, but Soda Pop started to feel poorly.

"Well, it can't be the toothpaste," said Soda Pop, "because I eat loads of that every day. I don't know what it can be…"

He was feeling worse every minute.

"You'll have to go home now, hotdog man," he said. "Can't you see I'm sick?" He felt so faint that he had to turn off the pop music.

The hotdog man coaxed two sluggish, half-painted tigers to come along with him and set off for home. Meanwhile, Soda Pop tapped a few fives on the telliphone and far away a doctor answered.

"I'm sick, I'm too tired to listen to pop music and my teeth are chattering," explained Soda Pop.

"Distemper with scarlet fever," said the doctor, and hung up.

"That's what dogs get, distemper," said Soda Pop to Mazarin. "I'm done for. Tomorrow I'll be barking and burying bones. You'd better put me on a leash so I don't run away!"

Distemper with Scarlet Fever

Next morning, Mazarin was woken by the sound of barking in the kitchen. Soda Pop was bounding about on all fours.

"Oh dear, have you got distemper?" cried Mazarin.

"Woof," said Soda Pop, flattening his ears.

"Can't you talk any more?"

"Yap, yap." Soda Pop jumped up to lick him on the face.

Then Mazarin realized Soda Pop was in a pretty bad way. He was scarlet too, his ears glowing like a couple of red traffic lights.

Mazarin only had to hurl himself at the front door a couple of times before it opened. Soda Pop flew out like an arrow and started scrabbling and digging up bones. He was really naughty as well, and wouldn't come when he was called.

"What shall I do?" Mazarin wondered. "I'll ask Dartanyong."

He hurried off to knock on Dartanyong's door.

There was no answer, so he opened it and went in. There was nobody home. The place was in a terrible mess and the bed looked like a battlefield, with the sheets and covers in one great tangle. Dartanyong was nowhere to be seen, but under the bed was a big, well-gnawed bone.

Mazarin was pretty worried because Dartanyong didn't usually go missing for more than five minutes at a time. He ran outside and started to call and look for him.

The giraffe woke up and bolted into the forest, and Soda Pop dug a hole in the lawn, sending soil spraying up.

Mazarin looked in the dilapidated old shed and the swimming pool, in the henhouse and the main house, and at last he found

Dartanyong crouched low behind the rubbish heap, sneaking up on an empty sauce bottle.

"Why are you creeping up on that old bottle?" said Mazarin.

Dartanyong looked up and growled.

"Aren't you the master painter?" said Mazarin.

"Woof," snapped Dartanyong, and tried to bite Mazarin's leg.

What a disaster. Dartanyong thought he was a dog too!

At that moment Soda Pop came lolloping up and they both went crazy, running around the lawn, then through all the rooms of the house. Dartanyong was so wild with excitement he started eating Soda Pop's slippers, which were lying in the hall, and Soda Pop found an old galosh, which he chewed into little bits.

Before long they were both awfully thirsty. They came out into the kitchen and wagged their tails. Mazarin poured water

78

into a big bowl on the floor. When they had splashily lapped it up there was a knock at the door and in came Gustav the robber. Soda Pop and Dartanyong threw themselves at him, biting his legs. They could tell by his smell that he was a robber. Gustav was shaken, and he kicked out to make them let go.

"Have they flipped?" he asked Mazarin. "Here's me, trying to be nice and hand back the brass knobs, and all I get for my trouble is to be jumped on and have my leg bitten off."

"Soda Pop caught distemper with scarlet fever last night, and this morning Dartanyong thinks he's a dog as well."

Gustav found this hilarious.

"In that case, let's train them a bit," he said. "I had a dog myself, so I know how to do it."

They all went outside because Gustav said the lawn was the best place for training.

First he tried to train them to heel beside him. But that was impossible because Dartanyong kept scratching himself and all Soda Pop wanted to do was dig holes. Then he tried to train them to run after a stick and bring it back in their mouths.

"Fetch the stick!" he said. "Fetch the stick, it's over there!"

Soda Pop and Dartanyong hunted and hunted but they couldn't find it.

In the end Gustav had to go and point it out, then Dartanyong raced up and grabbed it, and buried it at top speed behind the rubbish heap.

"Bother, they just don't get it," sighed Gustav. "Shall we try to teach them to jump through burning hoops?"

Mazarin didn't think that was a good idea. He was sure they'd both get stuck.

"Shall we train them to walk on two legs, then?" said Gustav.

"They can already do that, you cloth-head," said Mazarin.

In the meantime, Dartanyong and Soda Pop ran down to Dartanyong's running track and started sniffing at trees and lampposts. Dartanyong sniffed and sniffed, then suddenly lifted both legs at once and fell into a little heap on the ground. Gustav and Mazarin laughed so hard their tummies ached.

Then the cross old man came down the road, bellowing.

"My best iron bedstead!" he yelled. "He's taken it! The giraffe!"

He was in such a rage that he hardly noticed Soda Pop and Dartanyong nipping at his legs.

But then he stiffened and looked at them icily.

"What's the meaning of this?" he demanded. "Biting an old man's legs!"

Soda Pop and Dartanyong flattened their ears and growled menacingly.

"They think they're dogs," whispered Mazarin.

"Have you paid for their dog registrations?" the cross old man retorted, quick as a flash. "And are you keeping them on the leash? Remember, it's hunting season! Hah, I thought as much! A matter for the police, I reckon. I'll call the clink tonight!"

"Fine, and I shall answer," said Gustav. "I'm going back there shortly."

"That pestilential giraffe!" yelled the cross old man. "I tell you, if he eats my bed you'll owe me a fifty, no more, no less. And a floral mattress and a bedspread with a little coffee stain at one end."

"Does it have to be a coffee stain?" asked Mazarin. "We've just run out of coffee."

"Bedspread with coffee stain," insisted the cross old man. "Good afternoon!"

Gustav gave up trying to train Soda Pop and Dartanyong. They were simply hopeless.

"Maybe they're tracker dogs," he said to Mazarin. "Shall we get them to track down the cross old man's bed?"

Mazarin nodded.

"Sniff out the cross old man's bed," Gustav instructed them. "It's bound to be up in the forest somewhere."

Dartanyong and Soda Pop sniffed and scrabbled and all at once they tore off towards the forest and disappeared.

Four hours later they brought back a bed leg and a chewed-up pillow, which they buried at once behind the rubbish heap.

Gustav had left a while earlier for the jail, where they served chocolate pudding with whipped cream and raspberry jam until four o'clock at the latest.

Mazarin didn't know what to do with the two of them. They had caught the scent of the tigers, as well, and spent ages creeping about, lying in wait and yelping outside the barn.

"Just watch out, because if you sneak in there they'll gobble you up on the spot," said Mazarin.

Just then the hotdog man turned up on his cycle cart loaded with hotdogs.

Soda Pop and Dartanyong threw themselves at the hotdogs and started wolfing them down. The hotdog man looked in dismay from one to the other. He had no idea what was going on until Mazarin explained.

"Well, I'll just chuck the tigers these hotdogs, as promised," he said. "And I'd like to take another couple with me, because mine have run away again. But keep a firm hold on Mister Dartanyong and Soda Pop while I open the door."

He opened the barn door just a crack, tipped up the cart so the hotdogs poured inside, and quickly shut it again.

Soda Pop and Dartanyong barked like crazy when the scent of tiger wafted out.

The hotdog man waited until the tigers had eaten their fill and fallen asleep in untidy heaps before he opened the door again, manhandled two tigers onto his cart and set off for home. Soda

Pop and Dartanyong chased after him all the way, barking their heads off.

Evening fell and towards seven they came back home, dog-tired, with their tails between their legs. Dartanyong fell fast asleep under the garden table while Soda Pop sniffed about half-heartedly under the lilac hedge. Mazarin went over and scratched him behind the ears.

"Will you be yourself again soon, Soda Pop?" he asked.

A sound was coming from Soda Pop, soft as soft, and he had to bend right down to hear it:

"Come to me and kiss me slowly, gently, lovely," sang Soda Pop, and then: "Hold me, whisper my name, tell me who you are…"

Then he gave a few growls and fell asleep.

But Mazarin was delighted, because he knew that Soda Pop was on the mend!

Shocky Poodling
and Cripped Weem

By the next morning, Soda Pop had stopped thinking he was a dog. Mazarin had got so used to Soda Pop barking and growling, he jumped every time Soda Pop spoke.

"Did I really bite the cross old man's leg?" Soda Pop sniggered. "And Gustav's?" He had forgotten it all during the night.

"And you sniffed at everything and bounded about and growled and buried bones," said Mazarin.

"What did Dartanyong say about that?" Soda Pop was curious.

"Dartanyong thought he was a dog too, so he just barked, the same as you," said Mazarin.

Soda Pop started to shake with laughter.

"Hoho, how funny he must have looked!" he shrieked.

"Yes, he looked really funny," said Mazarin.

"I hope he still thinks he's a dog today," giggled Soda Pop. "Shall we go and see?"

They knocked at the woodshed and went in. Dartanyong was fast asleep and snoring, with only a bit of his hair sticking out of bed.

"There's a good dog! Go to your basket!" shouted Soda Pop.

Startled from sleep, Dartanyong sat up like a shot and stared at them wildly.

"What basket?" he muttered. "Can't a man lie in his own bed these days?"

"Oh, Dartanyong, it's you, is it?" said Soda Pop cautiously.

Dartanyong gave him a bewildered look.

"Dartanyong—never heard the name before!" he said.

"So whom do I have the pleasure of addressing?" Soda Pop asked.

"The name's Rockdart," said Dartanyong. "I'm a pop singer and I go on tour and do concerts all over the place."

"What luck!" yelled Soda Pop, leaping in the air. "Now we can form a pop band. I'm on electric guitar!"

"No, I play electric guitar," said Dartanyong. "And I sing and play the mouth organ at the same time."

"Well, so do I," said Soda Pop, "but I play drums as well, and anything else I can lay my hands on."

"Let's meet on the lawn at quarter past eleven," said Dartanyong. "I'll make my preparations in the meantime."

Mazarin and Soda Pop went into the house.

"Listen to him, going all snooty like that," muttered Soda Pop. "'I'll make my preparations' indeed!"

Soda Pop and Mazarin put on their usual old bathrobes and tea cosy hats and Soda Pop made an electric guitar from a broken pastry board and a lamp flex.

He still had a few drums from his younger days. They were in excellent shape, the skins only punctured in three places.

They'd found a little dust-covered organ in a wardrobe, which Mazarin dragged outside.

They sat on the organ as they waited for Dartanyong.

Finally the woodshed door creaked open and out stepped Dartanyong. He was so flashily dressed, they hardly recognized him. He had a bright red jacket with tight, yellowy green trousers, hair swept forward over his eyes, sideburns and a guitar with five white, six-watt plugs.

"Okay, here we go." Dartanyong tapped his foot to mark time.

They sang and played, giving it their very best shot. First they sang "You are the best thing I've got" and then "Hold me, whisper my name" followed by "Come to me and kiss me slowly" and "Love is golden, golden" and Dartanyong knew them all, or at least the first few words.

The last one—"I'm so sorry I have to go"—was too sad for Dartanyong. He started to snivel and sob, so they decided to take a break.

"Shall we go for a little walk?" asked Mazarin.

So they did.

They went along the running track past the mailboxes. They

took it for granted they'd have no letters so they didn't bother looking in theirs, but they lifted the lid of the cross old man's. And the red owls were nestled inside! There were at least five now and they looked really cute. The smallest one was no bigger than a dessert spoon.

"If I was the cross old man, I'd be delighted to have owls in my mailbox," said Soda Pop.

At that very moment the cross old man came along with a peculiar-looking parcel under his arm.

Mazarin was nervous. Would there be a big kerfuffle about

the bed the giraffe had gobbled up and the bedspread with the coffee stain and all that?

But strangely enough, the cross old man didn't say a word about any of that.

"Good day to you all," he said. "I expect you're wondering what's in this parcel? Well, you'll soon see. I'll unwrap the paper, like this, then fold up this layer of material, and pull out that one. And I'll fold out this wooden leg, and the other one, and this one and that one, there we are. And I'll slot this bit here, and wrap that around there, and look, ladies and gentlemen…"

Soda Pop and Mazarin and Dartanyong gaped wide-eyed as the cross old man busily unfolded one thing after the other until, hey presto, there was a huge bed blocking the track.

"Good night, good night." The cross old man snuggled down in the bed and pulled the cover over his ears.

"Good night," said Mazarin, Soda Pop and Dartanyong.

Then the cross old man stuck his head out again and gave them a searching look.

"So you're not dogs today, then?" he said. "You haven't bitten my leg once."

"No. We're pop singers today," said Soda Pop. "Allow me to introduce Rockdart, pleased to meet you."

They started playing their hearts out and Dartanyong sent shivers down their spines singing "As long as you keep on loving, you stay young."

But the cross old man threw himself back on his folding bed and pulled the cover over his head.

"GOOD NIGHT!" he shouted. "GET LOST!"

Just as they reached their own front yard the hotdog man turned up lugging his cycle cart again.

"There, there, down boy, sit," he said anxiously when he saw Dartanyong and Soda Pop.

"Don't give us that," said Soda Pop. "We're not dogs today, we're pop singers."

"Oh, then I shan't disturb you," said the hotdog man. "I was just dropping by to fetch two more tigers because the two I took yesterday have run off too!"

"Help yourself to as many as you like. I'm getting tired of tigers," said Soda Pop.

The hotdog man hung about outside the barn for nearly half an hour until he was sure they were all asleep. Then he pushed the cycle cart inside, loaded two tigers onto it and zipped off home.

"He can take the whole lot," Soda Pop said generously. "Tigers aren't fun any more. We could get hold of a few other animals to keep here instead. What do you think, Mazarin?"

Then Dartanyong decided they should go to the room that used to be red and record themselves performing.

"We'll be like a proper pop band," said Dartanyong. "We'll be able to play the recording and not have to bother playing ourselves."

Well, that was ingenious, no doubt about it, and it seemed the only thing to do. But first they needed a sound check, said Soda Pop, or it would sound terrible. He twiddled the knobs and coughed into a little microphone with an extremely long lead. With a bit more twiddling and coughing, a green light started flashing.

"Ladies and gentlemen, if you don't mind, I'll be off now…" Soda Pop announced.

"Hey, hang on, we were about to play our songs," grumbled Dartanyong.

"This is just the sound check, you dimwit," said Soda Pop. "And it's your turn!"

Dartanyong suddenly lost his nerve. All he could come up with was "Baa Baa Black Sheep," which he sang so out of tune that a red light started flashing on the machine.

Mazarin did his sound check with "When I'm Sixty-four," and then they were ready for the real recording.

They performed all their pop songs straight through in one go, then repeated them for good measure. It left them totally worn out and Dartanyong's sideburns all over the place.

Soda Pop had such a craving for chocolate pudding that he almost keeled over, but he knew there was only one packet in the pantry, which wasn't enough for three. It would just do for him and Mazarin.

"Listen Mazarin," he said, "how about a bit of shocky poodling and cripped weem?"

And he winked so hard his eyelids almost stuck together.

"What's that, cripped weem? What the dickens is he talking about?" said Dartanyong.

"Shocky poodling and cripped weem," Soda Pop repeated, winking wildly at Mazarin and treading hard on his toes.

Dartanyong shook his head crossly.

"Shocky poodling and cripped weem?" Mazarin murmured.

"Exactly," said Soda Pop encouragingly. "Just enough for two!"

Mazarin got it at last.

"Ah, right, shocky poodling and cripped weem!" he exclaimed. "Yes, please."

So they sneaked off to the golden bathroom and whipped up a glorious chocolate pudding, and before Dartanyong had even noticed them gone they'd gobbled the lot and come back, full up and very pleased with themselves.

Then they played the tape, and they actually sounded great,

especially Dartanyong whose voice quavered perfectly at the weepy bits.

But once the last song had faded away for the second time they heard a crackle from the microphone and Soda Pop's voice saying, "How about a bit of shocky poodling and cripped weem?"

Then Dartanyong's grumble: "What's that, cripped weem? What the dickens is he talking about?"

They listened to the whole tape over and over and each time they got to shocky poodling and cripped weem, Soda Pop and Mazarin shrieked with laughter.

But Dartanyong shook his head until his sideburns stood on end and before long he took himself home to the woodshed with the electric guitar under his arm.

Scorpion Barrels and Lingonberry Cases

Soda Pop and Mazarin were having breakfast as usual one morning. Yogurt with heaps of sugar and crunchy flakes, including the collector cards that came with them.

And Soda Pop chomped his way through a few eggs still in their shells, because funnily enough the shell is where all the vitamins are. And he read the paper and listened to some pop music and was very content with life.

Mazarin sat there quietly cutting twenty slices of cheese, which he carefully piled into a tower on his bread.

"Why aren't you saying anything? And why aren't you eating anything?" Soda Pop finally asked.

"I started thinking about barrels of scorpions," said Mazarin. "Just think if you stumbled on a barrel of scorpions!"

"Heck, that would be disgusting."

This made Mazarin jump.

"What's up with you—heck isn't a swear word, is it?" said Soda Pop.

"No," said Mazarin, "not really."

"So why did you jump then?" said Soda Pop.

"I don't know." Mazarin went on slicing cheese.

"But scorpion barrels sound interesting," said Soda Pop. "After all, someone might happen to stumble on a scorpion barrel this very day."

"I wonder what they look like," said Mazarin.

"Something tells me scorpion barrels are green," said Soda Pop. "But if you like, we can nip up to the forest and hunt for one."

They kicked the door open at once and set off. It was quite a mild, fine day. The pike were squeaking their heads off in the swimming pool and you could have heard a pin drop in the barn.

"They're not bad at all, these trees and clumps of grass and stuff," said Soda Pop, looking about him. He generally had these little nature-loving crazes a couple of times each summer.

"And look at the sky!" he cried ecstatically. "It's so big it's amazing!"

At that moment, Dartanyong came limping out of the woodshed.

"Good morning. Who am I speaking to?" shouted Soda Pop.

"Do you need spectacles, or what?" snapped Dartanyong. "I'm Dartanyong, your father."

"Aha, how are you then, Dartanyong?" said Soda Pop.

"Absolutely dreadful," grumbled Dartanyong. "Dizzy spells, hot flushes and two mosquito bites on my left ear. I'll bandage them up as soon as this hot flush has passed."

"Can I give you a bit of advice?" said Soda Pop. "Grow those sideburns again. They really suited you."

Dartanyong shook his head. Sideburns for an old man! He'd never heard anything so ridiculous.

"If anybody asks for us, we're out hunting," said Soda Pop. "For scorpion barrels."

They took a short cut across the field of oats and were soon in the forest where the hunt could begin.

But first, Soda Pop thought they should do the run to Dartanyong's grandpa and back, to make sure they were fit. Dartanyong's grandpa was sitting in his pine tree and cuckooed as they reached him, but his beak fell when they merely shouted "Good morning!" and turned and sprinted on their way.

"We'll bring you seeds on Christmas Eve. Maybe!" yelled Soda Pop, still sore about being nagged to get a job last time they were there.

Mazarin crossed the finish line five paces ahead, but Soda Pop claimed he'd won anyway.

"But I was first," complained Mazarin.

"That's a matter of judgment," said Soda Pop, not caring two hoots. "Seen from the air and with poor eyesight, we crossed the finishing line at exactly the same time. And anyway, I'm senior and what's more it's my running track. I made it."

"But I came first," persisted Mazarin.

"We both came first. It's important to stick together, remember that," said Soda Pop. "Now let's say no more about it."

Then they began hunting in earnest for scorpion barrels.

They had to hunt for a very long time, because the whole place was teeming with mushrooms and toadstools and ant heaps and foxes and woodpeckers, making it tricky to see if there were scorpion barrels or not. And they kept forgetting what they were looking for and charged around instead with bendy sticks in their mouths pretending to be rhinoceroses.

When they came to a huge rock they took a break. They climbed to the top and sat down, and Soda Pop sang "You've deserted me again and my nerves can't take the strain…" so loud that Dartanyong's grandpa started cuckooing wildly in his pine tree.

They set off again and behind a big fir tree they bumped straight into Gustav.

"What are you doing here—are you on break?" asked Soda Pop in surprise.

Yes, Gustav really had been given a week's break, so he was out picking lingonberries, he said.

"But are there lingonberries in this forest?" asked Soda Pop. He'd never seen them growing there, at any rate.

"Of course, they're all over the place if you just look down," said Gustav.

"Are you gathering them in suitcases, man?" Soda Pop gave Gustav's brown suitcases a curious look.

"You said it. That's exactly what I'm doing," said Gustav. "By the way, if you feel like being a dog again we could do a bit more training. Do you remember biting me in the leg, incidentally?"

No, Soda Pop couldn't remember that, but it must have been hilarious. "Can we have a look at your berries?" he said, with a secret wink to Mazarin.

No, these were the kind of lingonberry that faded from red to white if you looked at them for too long, Gustav said. And that would never do.

So they said a quick goodbye and carried on with their hunt. But they must have been unusual berries Gustav had found, because they made a terrible clanking as he walked away.

"I'll give you a taste once I've made them into jam, ho ho ho," hollered Gustav before disappearing among the trees.

"I don't care what he's taken, as long as he hasn't got my brass knobs again," said Soda Pop. "Right, let's get on with it. What were we hunting for?"

"Scorpion barrels," said Mazarin.

Here and there in the moss they came across old bed legs and moth-eaten blankets the giraffe had abandoned, and in a little daisy meadow they found the cross old man, who had put up his bed and was fast asleep and snoring with his thermos of coffee beside him.

The giggly pair tiptoed about a bit and charged around a bit more, but nothing woke the cross old man. Just for fun they unscrewed the top of his thermos and poured a little coffee, which came out palest brown, exactly the sort of top-quality wishy-washy coffee they'd expected.

"Yuck. He can drink this dishwater himself." Soda Pop poured it back into the flask.

They belted out "Hold me, whisper my name" until the cross old man leapt out of bed like a raging lion.

"Shove off. You're driving me mad. GET LOST!" he yelled.

"We were only trying to warn you about the scorpion barrels," Soda Pop said gently. "There could easily be one under your bed."

The cross old man leaped into action, folding up his bed and tucking his thermos under his arm.

"Where?" He looked around in alarm.

Soda Pop and Mazarin simply walked on, leaving the cross old man squatting with his thermos on the folded bed.

Strangely, there seemed to be a great scarcity of scorpion barrels in that particular forest, but there were plenty of old pine cones and oodles of sticks and twigs lying around. Soda Pop ran about flapping his bathrobe and frightening the living daylights out of the birds nearby.

Before they knew it they came to the tree where Dartanyong's grandpa lived.

Soda Pop stopped short and put a finger to his lips.

"Shhh," he said. "Don't move, Mazarin! Look at the ground, right beside the pine tree. A scorpion barrel!"

And yes, it really was a scorpion barrel! Green, with a hoop around its belly, and the lid on, thank goodness.

Soda Pop picked up a long stick and gave the lid a poke to see if the barrel was dangerous. Dartanyong's grandpa nearly screeched his head off, but they couldn't make out the words. After a few pokes, the scorpion barrel came to life and suddenly raised its lid. But it wasn't a scorpion barrel at all. It was Dartanyong in his green tracksuit and hunter's hat!

Dartanyong didn't think much of Soda Pop poking his head with a stick.

He got even grumpier when he heard he'd been mistaken for a scorpion barrel.

"I come up here with seeds for Grandpa, hoping for a bit of peace and quiet, and you turn up drivelling on about scorpion barrels. Hmph, my head's buzzing horribly!" He snuggled up against the pine tree and went back to sleep.

"Bang bang!" yelled Soda Pop, aiming his stick at Dartanyong's grandfather, then he and Mazarin ran away as fast as they could.

It was dusk when they got home. Gustav was sitting resting on the edge of the swimming pool in his fish trunks with the perch pattern. The pictures they'd drawn on his tummy and legs had faded, so he must have been in the pool a very long time. The suitcases stood at the side of the track. Soda Pop lifted one and nearly gave himself lumbago, it was so heavy.

"Heavy lingonberries you've got in here, Gustav!" he called.

"Yes, they're magnificent specimens!" Gustav called back.

"Gustav, have you been to see Dartanyong today?" shouted Soda Pop.

"Yes, I looked in for a minute a while ago, but he wasn't home," said Gustav.

So Soda Pop and Mazarin thought they'd better drop by Dartanyong's woodshed too. Everything looked the same as usual, but the cups for triple jump and butterfly stroke were missing. The silver spoons had gone too, funnily enough, and a disgusting old coffee pan so old it was worth a fortune. Soda Pop and Mazarin went and sat beside Gustav.

"Could I have a look in your suitcases, Gustav?" Soda Pop pushed back his tea cosy to look him in the eye.

"A few old berries are no big deal, are they?" said Gustav.

"Please, nice Gustav," said Soda Pop.

Well, Gustav couldn't resist that.

"Okay, let's go down and open them, and you'll see lingon-berries like you've never seen before!"

Click, click, Gustav opened up the suitcases, and silver spoons and coffee pans and cups for butterfly stroke came tumbling out.

"Would you look at that!" exclaimed Gustav clapping his hands. "And there was I thinking they were full of berries!"

"Gustav, Gustav," said Soda Pop. "Put the spoons and stuff back in the woodshed now, otherwise you'll upset Dartanyong. He's compiled long lists of everything, you know."

"Oh no, he's not getting all of it," said Gustav indignantly. "I pinched some of it from the cross old man and some from the hotdog man. And some I picked up at home, at the jail."

After a bit of a think he put some things back in the woodshed, and together they closed the suitcases so Gustav could carry on with his little trip, as he put it.

The minute Gustav was gone, the hotdog man turned up with his cycle cart. "It's me again," he puffed. "I've come to get another two tigers, because the ones I took last time have run away as well."

"Be my guest: go for it." Soda Pop helped him to unlock the barn door. But then things went a bit wrong, because the door flew open and out flowed a never-ending stream of tigers.

Soda Pop pressed himself flat to the barn door and pretended not to exist, while Mazarin managed a last-minute scramble up to the swimming pool. The hotdog man fell to the ground in a faint and the tigers went flying over him in long, elegant leaps and one by one vanished into the forest.

Finally the yard was empty and quiet again. The hotdog man woke from his faint and Soda Pop started giggling hysterically.

"Tell you what, let's take a dip, eh?" He climbed up and dived head first into the swimming pool. By the time he resurfaced he was pretty much himself again. Then finding an ancient bar of chocolate in his pocket put him in excellent spirits.

"Give me a moment to dry off," he called to the hotdog man and Mazarin, and he sat down under the apple tree to enjoy the chocolate in peace.

Mazarin and the hotdog man realized at once what he was up to and dashed over to join him.

"Give us a taste, give us a taste," they shouted.

"No, and I'll tell you why," said Soda Pop. "There's onion in it. I've never known such revolting chocolate. Simply disgusting!" And he ate it all up.

"You two are lucky you didn't have to eat it," he said, licking his lips.

So the hotdog man had to go home without any tigers for once, and the barn looked all sad and empty with only a few loose tiger tails left in the straw.

Mazarin and Soda Pop went down to the rubbish heap and patted the giraffe because they'd forgotten all about him recently. Then they went inside and switched on the tape recorder and Soda Pop made his signature meal in a saucepan. It was quite tricky to make. You had to mix together crackers and eggs and old porridge and a bit of mashed potato, a few lingonberries and milk, and then it was ready. Mazarin would have to make do with ice cream, said Soda Pop, because there was only enough of his special dish for one. Just so Mazarin knew.

When they'd finished their meal and had played *shocky poodling and cripped weem* at least thirty times, Soda Pop felt another nature-loving craze coming on and dashed outside. It was quite dark because it was evening.

"Look at the trees," he cried, in raptures. "And listen to the birds!"

And if you listened carefully, you could actually hear a bird sighing in a tree.

"What could it be?" asked Soda Pop. "Must be an owl."

He crept towards it, eyes peeled. Now and then another sigh came from the tree.

"I can't wait, I have to know what it is." Soda Pop shook the tree, and carried on shaking until a startled thrush fell out, legs sticking in the air.

That was the end of Soda Pop's interest in nature and he went back inside to Mazarin.

"Put the shocky poodling on, if you wouldn't mind," he said. "It's been a taxing day. Phew."

While he waited for Mazarin to whip up the pudding, Soda Pop threw himself down under the kitchen table and started to hum the tune "Come to me..."